PRAISE FOR
"NUMBER SEVENTY-FIVE"

With an attention to detail, and a slowly building sense of dread and horror, Ashley Fontainne's "Number Seventy-Five" will have you racing through her story of online connection, and just how bad things can go on a date. This is a tale with its Hitchcockian twists dealing with greed and murder, I dare you to stop reading.

~ Matthew Costello, author of "Vacation" and "Home"~

Ashley Fontainne proves with "Number Seventy-Five" that she's a talent to watch.

~ Raymond Benson, author of The Black Stiletto series ~

Stephen King owns the horror genre, and John Grisham owns legal thrillers, but Ashley Fontainne has created her own genre that is just as intense, *The Evil Bitches Thriller*. Fontainne is back again with a neck snapping, jaw dropping thriller you will not be able to put down. "Number Seventy-Five" had me at the first page and dragged me mercilessly along. I was unable to put it down. I had to put everything on hold to finish it in one reading and to be honest I was disappointed it was not much longer. No one captures the evil twisted mentality of a female sociopath better than Fontainne. Her characters are believable, real, and evil beyond belief.

~ Zach Fortier, author of "Curbchek" and "Street Creds"

ASHLEY FONTAINNE

NUMBER SEVENTY-FIVE

RMSW PRESS

Cover, interior book design and eBook design
by One of a Kind Covers
www.oneofakindcover.wix.com/oneofakind

Edited by Jeff LaFerney

NUMBER SEVENTY-FIVE

Copyright © 2013 Ashley Fontainne

Published by
RMSW Press

ISBN-13: 978-0615786773
ISBN-10: 0615786774

Visit the author at:
Website:
www.ashleyfontainne.com
Blog:
www.ramblingsofamadsouthernwoman.blogspot.com
Facebook:
www.facebook.com/ashleyfontainne
Twitter:
@AshleyFontainne
Goodreads:
www.goodreads.com/author/show/4958072.Ashley_Fontainne

For everyone searching for love online...
be careful what you wish for.

THE BEGINNING

THE SMELL OF decaying earth filled my nostrils with a toxic stench, coaxing me slowly out of the darkness. Confusion poked at every corner of my mind like sharp talons and nearly made me gasp from their burning grip. My body woke up next and sent its own signals of torment speeding through my neurons up to my fuzzy brain. Every inch of me throbbed with white, searing pain. My ears joined the sensory overload fray and sent a signal of grating, metallic scraping sounds that came from behind me. The odd familiarity of the noise tried to take center stage in my thoughts but failed miserably. The struggle against numerous others clamored over it with ease.

The heavy fog of confusion was instantaneously burned away by the jolt of adrenaline that flushed out my system from its prior fugue state. My aching body reacted by stiffening, my mind controlled now by ingrained gut instincts which forced me to remain frozen in place like hidden prey. Memories burst forth in sharp succession and showered me with the last images of consciousness I could conjure up. My mind clamored to put the broken pieces together.

CHAPTER 1

LIKE A GIDDY schoolgirl, I primped and preened in front of the unforgiving mirror. I changed ensembles ten times before I settled on the ideal outfit which consisted of a pair of dark blue jeans, a white T-shirt and my brown riding boots. A bland choice but the one I was most comfortable in, which was really all that mattered. The pile of discarded clothes on my bed almost made me forget that I was in my forties. When I slid the mid-calf boots on, I laughed at myself since it was damn near summertime, but they were the only thing in my closet that had a heel and looked somewhat dressy.

The words of my best friend, Shawna, hung over me while I applied a minimal amount of makeup and finished fluffing my dishwater-blonde hair. Shawna had made me promise to call her when I made it home afterward and dish to her eager ears all the juicy details of the upcoming evening. My nervous laughter had tittered across the phone lines when she teased me about my timid excursion into the dating world. After all, three long years of playing the role of a bitter single woman was enough, she had said.

I made a quick phone call to secure dinner reservations at the eloquent yet affordable Chancery Court, which was over thirty miles from my hometown in Bainsville. It was a quaint, southern restaurant frequented by cops, which conveyed a safe haven...a neutral meeting ground. It also put my worried friend at ease since I would be surrounded by a sea of blue.

I winced when I noticed more gray hairs and wished I would have had time to hit the beauty parlor. My once vibrant locks desperately needed an update. Getting older sucked; that was for sure. Oh well, it was too late now. I would just have to be satisfied with what God gave me, and so would my date.

I pecked out a text message on my cellphone screen to Shawna that read "escape," ready to send if I needed the cavalry to come rescue me should anything go awry during the date. That was Shawna's last instruction to me before I had disconnected our call earlier after I told her that I would never make it to dinner if she didn't hush. That girl was always planning ahead for everything and all unseen scenarios.

After one last perfunctory glimpse in the mirror I was off, full of anxious jitters. I was about to meet for the very first time the man I had been conversing with online for several weeks. While I drove to the restaurant, Shawna's heavy, Tennessee lilt began replaying in my head. Like a broken record, it repeated over and over: "Safety first, Mandy. Your momma didn't raise no fool anymore than mine did. A true woman is prepared for anything, especially a southern one, 'cause we know the woods is full of varmints."

"Damn straight, girl. That's why my gun's sittin' inside my purse. You know I'm a good shot and not afraid to take aim if necessary," I had replied.

Shawna had laughed and told me I was being overly cautious, but I told her in this day and age, a single woman couldn't be too careful. Especially one like me that only stood five foot two…equalizers were a necessity in the violent world we lived in. It seemed like I couldn't turn on the news without a report about a missing woman and I had no desire to ever be in that category.

A sketchy smile at the memory crossed my face, thankful that I had taken all the necessary precautions. Jacob did not have my home address, my personal telephone number, or the name of my employer. We were meeting in a public place on my terms, not his. I let my friends and family know where we planned on dining and promised to call them all once I was on my way home.

Shawna even insisted the location of our first meeting be at the Chancery Court since her brother Samuel and his other cop buddies hung out there all the time. Even though Sam was on vacation, Shawna promised that she would contact him and make sure the place was crawling with gun-toting guards--each one ready, willing and able to watch my back if something seemed amiss. Such was the connection between cops and nurses.

I had been thankful that Samuel was out of town and wouldn't be one of the eyes watching me while on a date. Not only would I have been embarrassed for my childhood friend to know I was meeting someone that I met online, but it would have been awkward with him there since he still had feelings for me. What started out as puppy love for his older sister's closest companion segued over to something much deeper as Samuel became an adult. When he would bring a person in to the ER for a breathalyzer or to follow up on an accident, he followed me around like a shadow.

The seventeen years I had worked at the emergency room at Bainsville Mercy General garnered lasting friendships with local law enforcement. A few, including Samuel, got too friendly after my divorce, but once put in their place after some choice words were plucked out of my southern girl repertoire, they backed off. It was my love for the idle banter and deep camaraderie that kept me from resigning my position and moving to another venue. Working alongside my ex, the renowned Dr. Scott Russell, was like having a tooth constantly extracted. The pain was damned near unbearable, but my friends helped me through it.

Both nurses and cops worked the same grueling shifts and witnessed up front and personal the dark deeds that humans inflicted upon each other. Oftentimes, the disturbed laughter and pranks pulled seemed to be the only release valve that could be found to keep from going stark-raving mad. Each group was exposed to senseless violence every day. The bonds were for life, and I felt an invisible safety net around me, so I let my thoughts leave the preparation stage and float over to the meeting.

The anticipation of seeing if the constant communication the last six weeks with Jacob online might lead somewhere hit me next. At the same time, I feared that it could be worth pursuing and that it might not. My palms poured gallons of sweat as I gripped the wheel with ferocious intensity.

What if all of our conversations were a drummed up farce? What if I walked in and didn't recognize him? What if he took one look at me and ran out the door? Oh God, why did I ever let Shawna talk me into joining a freaking dating site?

I parked at the front entrance and willed my hands to stop shaking, wiping the dampness away on my jeans. All these crazy thoughts, self-doubt, and worry I had already played over a hundred times in my head before I ever agreed to our meeting. The pros and cons were weighed, and in the end, sheer curiosity won out. Determined to not let my normally jaded behavior win, I checked my reflection one last time in the review mirror and reached for my purse. The .22 was bulky and made an obvious bulge, so I decided not to scare the pants off my poor date and slid it inside my boot before stepping out into the night.

Hot, damp air greeted me as I exited, and I groaned in protest. I prayed my hair would stay in place and not become an enormous frizz ball before I made it through the front doors. I took a deep breath, grasped the door handle, and stepped inside.

Relief washed over me when Jacob rose from his seat in the waiting area. The face in front of me was different from his online profile…he was even more handsome in person. Thank God! His light-blonde hair hung just below his collar in soft waves. His dark-brown eyes were deeply set and huge and framed by black eyelashes. He was tall and well built, about six foot one. It was obvious he wasn't a natural blonde, which I found rather funny. I hadn't met very many men over the years who colored their hair, except for a few who washed the grays away. Seeing one who was a bottle blonde was rather comical and I had to force myself not to stare.

The first hurdle was cleared. At least he wasn't some disgusting troll, nor did he run when he realized that I looked exactly like my online photo. Guess I *was* still a looker at forty-one, at least according to Shawna.

We shared pleasant conversation over a delicious meal for the next two hours, the flirting kept at a minimal level as we eased through first date blunders. Our conversation huddled around easy topics of discussion: the weather, the Titans' chances for the next Super Bowl, the sweet yet messy ribs in front of us. Jacob's laugh was easy and light, his comments polite and not filled with underlying sexual innuendoes, which was a welcome change from my other interactions with men.

We each excused ourselves once during the date to retreat to the bathroom. When I took my turn, I used the time to send a quick text to Shawna and asked if she would please contact Sam and ask him to call the deputy dogs off. The place was packed with familiar faces and I felt like a fish in a bowl while Jacob and I ate. When it was Jacob's turn to use the facilities, while I sipped the cool iced tea, I wondered if he was texting someone too since he was gone longer than I had been.

When the evening drew to a close and Jacob asked if I wanted to go walk around town, I saw a hint of sadness when my response to his question was in the negative. Like the gentlemen I had come to know online, he walked me to my car and our evening ended with an awkward yet tender brush of his heated lips against my cool ones. The bland kiss was followed by hushed promises from him in my ear to meet again. With a disinterested glance, I watched him saunter back to his truck.

The cool leather seat of my car embraced my warm body, and I settled in for the drive home, filled with a rush of emotions that battled for control. Could I, *should* I, let my life be controlled by my lonely heart? That game had already been played and I lost my ass right along with my heart. Scott and I had been high school sweethearts and married the summer after graduation. I went to nursing school first; then supported us financially while he went to med school. Unable to bear children, our lives centered around our home, our friends, and various charities. Apparently that wasn't enough for Scott because he discovered a new hobby in our fifteenth year of marital bliss…bed hopping.

After two years of painful counseling and shattered promises to remain faithful, I had had enough. I had been devastated, my spirit crushed. It took two years after our divorce for me to stop mentally castrating every male who came within ten feet of me and another one for my verbal assaults to end. My nasty attitude was quickly given a nickname by one cop after a thorough dressing down, and it spread like wildfire in a parched forest…"Maneater Mandy."

I didn't want to be a bitter woman any longer. I wanted to find someone to share my life with. A man who treated me as a partner, a best friend, a confidante… to walk through life holding hands and facing all the ups and down together as a united front. I wanted someone to sit on the porch with and admire the simple beauty of a sunrise or sunset in quiet awe. What my heart ached for was a gentle lover and a friend that tears and smiles could be shown to without fear of reprieve for being overly emotional.

While driving, I came to the conclusion that I *could* release my tight grip around my heart to love again… just not with Jacob Wilson. I couldn't quite put my finger on the exact reason, but the small poke in my gut told me he wasn't the one. Funny how online chemistry can be so deceptive because there were no real sparks flying between the two of us. I had been like a kid at the fireworks stand — all excited about the rocket purchased in hopes of seeing a vivid explosion of colors, but deflated when it fizzled out as a dud.

I called Shawna and my mother and told them I was on my way home. Shawna seemed shocked that I called her so early, a hint of disappointment in her voice at the date being over so soon. She begged me to divulge all the gossip, but I told her I would spill it when I returned home. The stretch of road I was on was about to turn curvy, and I wanted to maintain all my focus on the highway. Irritated, she told me I'd better before she hung up without another word.

I smiled at my first wade into the choppy waters of the dating world, unscathed and no worse for the wear. Even though this "love connection" wouldn't happen, it did give me hope that eventually it could with someone else. Lost in thought, I was brought back to reality by a loud *bang*. The steering wheel jerked in my hands and I almost lost control of the car. I eased it over to the side of the darkened blacktop and climbed out.

The examination, done in bitter distaste as I stepped out onto the empty road, proved my theory...a blown right tire. Great! Just dandy! It was a perfect end to a not-so-perfect evening. Shawna would appreciate the irony since she knew one thing I had always feared was being stuck on a dark road with a flat.

When I started back to the driver's door to retrieve my cell to call AAA, I almost called Shawna and asked her to send out a distress signal to the cops who had been spying on me all night long. Before I could dial, headlights shimmered in the distance--a welcome salvation for a stranded motorist.

A familiar vehicle approached and stopped, and the voice I didn't plan on hearing again anytime soon spoke as he stepped out of his truck.

"Well, hey Mandy. Fancy meeting you way out here. Looks like you need some help," Jacob said.

That's when I noticed the tire iron in his hand and that he wasn't heading for my blown tire.

He was heading straight toward me.

THE THUNDERCLAP OF rushing blood in my ears momentarily made me forget the jackhammering in my skull. Panic welled up inside of me, dangerously close to being expelled from my body in the form of an ear splitting scream. My blood coursed through me, but all I felt was the chill of fear. The old adage I had read in so many books and scoffed at throughout the years I unfortunately now knew was true. Fear froze the flowing crimson. Terror turned my veins into a conductor of the slushy red liquid.

The memories from earlier that had danced a disjointed waltz through my foggy head came together in one looming picture. What was created was a terrifying portrait of my deadly predicament. The realization that my body was painfully twisted in a heap atop the damp, hard ground made the scream lurk at the edges of my parched mouth. But what caused the fear to skitter up my aching spine was that I finally recognized the sounds coming from behind me.

The clanking of a shovel ripping through the earth intermingled with the light groans of labor from the digger. Someone was digging a grave, and I was overwhelmed with the terror that it was for my body.

No longer did I concern myself with how I came to be face down in reeking dirt. Built-in survival instincts overrode everything else. Driven by sheer terror and the will to survive, I felt the lights in all interior rooms in my mind flick off, and only one bulb remained. The brilliant glow pulled me inside its formidable walls.

Escape.

Live.

Freedom.

I dared not open my eyes to survey my surroundings. First, I needed to assess the pain that ripped through me with each breath. A cracked rib, perhaps two, but no punctured lung, judging by the absence of the telltale gurgles I had heard so many patients suffer over the years. I forced my training to take over and continued my assessment, starting with my head. I isolated the intense pain to my right side, which centered round my eye socket and cheekbone area. Whether produced from a direct hit or concussion impact from the hard ground did not matter.

My right arm was pinned beneath my body and when I forced a slight wiggle from my fingers, the stab of pain let me know that several were broken. My mental examination continued to my pelvis. Relief brushed over me only briefly when I noticed no pain emanated from there. Ending with my legs, the ember-hot pain in my right knee was a sure sign the kneecap was either broken or dislodged. Lastly, the dull throb from my left ankle was difficult to determine, although it felt like it rested on top of a sharp rock.

Panic clenched at my chest again when it became clear that I wasn't going to be able to jump up and run for my freedom. I forced the bile down that bubbled inside me and strained all my senses to focus on my foreign surroundings. The heavy digging still continued from behind me. Yet other than the grunts of air from my captor, I heard nothing else. No traffic. No bugs. No sounds of civilization. Not a single blip to help me figure out my location.

The small hairs on my exposed arms and face stood erect--a clear indicator that the temperature of the air was cold. This revelation added even more confusion to my situation. It was mid-May. I wanted to believe that the goose bumps were from the shock of injuries to my body, but the frosty air I inhaled told me a different story.

Oh God, where in the hell was I?

The smell that woke me up hit me again, the scent stronger being than before. I held a whimper of despair at bay when I recognized it…the stagnant, pungent aroma of decomposing flesh.

I tried to use every trick I'd ever been taught to retain my composure, but my body betrayed me and began to tremble in fear. Realizing I might only have seconds before it was noticed that I was awake, I forced my left eye to open and peered out from behind my dirt-encrusted eyelashes.

A faint glow of yellow didn't illuminate much, but it was enough to grasp the enormity of things. Shallow mounds of raised earth, more than I could count, faced me, each neatly dug in straight rows, identical in size and shape to the other. A mangled body was laid out on top of the freshly extracted dirt closest to me, the blood a dark shade of burgundy, signaling coagulation had begun. Although nearly every inch of the clothes it seeped out upon was covered, I recognized the outfit and the blonde hair. The whimper I held back for so long escaped when my eye forced my brain to comprehend what it was looking at.

Graves—with Jacob's body next in line for burial and most likely, followed by mine.

"Oh, you woke up. Sorry, Mandy. Guess Jacob didn't clock you as hard as I thought. I'll tell ya though, from my vantage point, it sure seemed like he did."

The sound of shoveling stopped, and I heard the crunch of the hardened earth under heavy soles as feet brought my faceless captor closer. The tears flowed faster when his dirt-covered boots stood in my direct line of vision and recognition of his voice hit home.

My thoughts were a muddled mass of questions and each jockeyed for control. *What the fuck was going on?* When I recognized the deep, baritone voice of Samuel coming from behind me, a rush of elation raced through me, but that glorious sensation was short lived. Other, more ominous thoughts took center stage. *How in the hell did he know Jacob's name? Why was Jacob's dead body in a bloody pile less than ten feet from me? Did Samuel kill him to save me? If so, why wasn't he helping me? Where was I? Most importantly, why the hell was he digging?*

A yelp of anguish erupted out of me when his cold hand reached down and touched my face. His filthy fingers slowly wiped at my tears. I heard a crack from his knees when he bent down and brought his familiar face inches from my own, his breath hot as it warmed my icy cheek.

"You weren't supposed to wake up, doll baby. God, I didn't want you to suffer, I really didn't. I hoped you'd just sleep forever, without any more pain. Poor girl, you were just at the wrong place at the wrong time."

Samuel stared down at my crumpled body while his hand caressed my knotted hair, his blue eyes full of madness and sympathy.

No longer did the fear of being noticed keep me still, so I gulped in a few pain-filled breaths of the frigid night air and spit out the grit and gravel that filled my mouth before I responded.

"Samuel, what are you talkin' about?" I asked, the words barely above a breathy whisper as they exited from my swollen throat.

He continued to stroke my hair, but the once gentle caresses were gone, replaced with the heaviness of anger. When he pulled his hand away, it was covered in my blood.

"I promise you, Mandy, I didn't have no idea you were his date tonight. Please, please believe that. When I saw you get out of your car at the restaurant and walk in, you got no idea how upset I was. *This* was the *night!* It's been planned for months now, and everything was set in motion just so. No turnin' back once the wheels started rollin', no siree Bob. There was no way I could stop. You understand, right?"

While he spoke, his blue orbs pleaded with mine for recognition that I did as tears of regret swam behind them.

"No, I guess you wouldn't. But that's okay. I'll explain it all to you while I finish up," Samuel said, rising to his feet and stepping behind me once more. I assumed he took my silence to his question as my answer.

"This was the end, the last one. I swear to it, as God almighty is my witness, Mandy. He didn't want to stop, but I told him in the beginnin' that seventy-five was the magic number. You don't know how much I wish it wasn't yours."

In the pain and terror-filled state I was in, my cheek still firmly pressed against the wet dirt, comprehending Sam's words was damn near impossible. However, I did detect a hint, a deep sadness, in his voice.

Number seventy-five? Last one? Last one, what?

The sound of the shovel as he snatched and flung more earth from its place started again. Each time the metallic end made contact with the hardened ground and dug the hole deeper, I felt the sensation travel through my nerves. The screeching neurons left me no doubt that I was awake and not experiencing a wicked nightmare. I forced myself to remain calm and keep him talking while I worked out the details of what could possibly be my last few moments alive.

The coolness of the night air helped dislodge the cobwebs from my head, but that feeling didn't last too long. The scent molecules that followed it made my stomach lurch in protest. My heart pounded in response to the stench of death.

"Samuel, please. Ribs are broken...trouble breathing," I gasped, hoping I could convince him to drop the shovel and at least help me move, buying me a few more precious minutes. Sure enough, the clang of the handle as it met with the ground rang through my ears. In a flash, he was in front of me once more.

"Oh Mandy, sorry. Should've helped you up before. Lots going on tonight and manners just slipped my mind. Guess I am not thinkin' clearly. This'll probably hurt. He roughed you up pretty bad before I got there. You put up a good fight, though. Got a few good licks in on him too, so you should be proud 'bout that, my li'l spitfire. You didn't go down without a good fight. And that's the Mandy I know and love. But don't worry, he can't hurt you, or anyone else, anymore. I made sure of that."

Sam's tattooed arms encircled my waist, and in one swift movement, he scooped my limp body, cradling me like a football under the crook of his right arm. I bit my lip so hard that I tasted the rusty flavor of my own blood to keep my screams from shooting out of me. He took a few careful steps before depositing me in the sitting position, my back pressed up against a damp, icy surface. He knelt down and wiped the bloody mass of hair from my face, his eyes backlit by the faint yellow light from the lantern that sat next to his silent shovel.

A dirty, blood encrusted shovel that rested right next to the freshly dug grave.

"There. That should be better. At least you aren't face down in the filth anymore. I'm sorry the cave wall is so cold though. Guess you should've worn a jacket, huh? But you looked really nice this evening, Mandy. Really, you did. Just as pretty as a picture."

His voice was tender, just like his fingers that smoothed my hair back, which allowed me to take in a full view of my prison for the first time. Once the white stars of pain disappeared from my vision, I followed the dim light and glanced around. My heart nearly stopped beating when full cognizance settled in—I *was* in a cave. One full of shallow grave mounds too numerous to count. My stare was locked onto the newest one that Jacob's crooked frame rested upon, his body not yet deposited into its final resting place.

Tears leaked out in response to excruciating pain of being moved.

"Now Mandy, don't cry. At least not for that evil vermin over there. He ain't worth it," Samuel said, his eyes settling upon the same spot as my own. "You should be thankin' me that I pulled up when I did. I stopped him before he did to you what he did with all the others. He was just loadin' you in his truck when I arrived. Had he taken you to his place…well, you don't want to know." His tone switched from tenderness to irritation as his hand swept the expanse of the endless shallow graves in front of us. "That's all his doin', not mine. Damn but he was a cruel, vicious bastard."

The tears flowed freely down my face, but not for the reasons my best friend's brother thought. They raced down and melded into the dirty cotton of my once white shirt and made a montage of patterns from the caked-on dirt. No, these tears were produced by stark reality. I was in hell and my means of escape were nil.

Confirmation of broken ribs, a dislocated kneecap, and three busted fingers on my right hand was made when Sam moved me. The dull throb increased in intensity from my left ankle. I had no idea how long I'd been unconscious. The throbbing in my temple and the memory of Jacob coming at me with the tire iron sped by, which meant I had a mild concussion. I prayed silently that my skull wasn't fractured.

I had no idea where I was, and neither did anyone else. The only thing I knew for sure was that Sam was digging my grave even though he didn't really seem to want to. But he wasn't stopping, either.

Something deep inside me reached invisible fingers up to my heart, and like the tentacles of an octopus, wrapped around it like a crushing vice. The tightness shut off all my emotional connections to the outside world. All of my attention needed to focus on Samuel, or as I had always called him, Sambo. My mind had always seen him as the quiet, shy boy who had tagged along with me and Shawna ever since I could remember. The loner who worshipped me from afar, his heart saddened when I got married and broken when I rejected his advances after my divorce. I needed to use those feelings to my advantage against him.

My best-friend's little brother who went from playing cops and robbers in their backyard to actually becoming a well-decorated and respected deputy. The quick smile and bland face that I knew so well now held me hostage and was about to bury me.

I refused to beg for my life. No way would I go out blubbering like some pathetic, half-clothed horror movie victim.

Not me.

Not Mandy Russell.

If this was to be my final stand, I would battle, tooth and nail, for every last breath.

I needed to keep him talking.

I needed to keep myself out of that fucking hole.

"MAY I?" I asked. I nodded my head and darted my eyes to the opened pack of cigarettes in Samuel's pocket.

"But Mandy, you quit," Samuel replied with a look of repugnance mixed with disapproval. His shocked expression nearly made me laugh. I stared at my child-hood friend and waited in silence. The dark blue eyes that looked back at me were a strange conglomeration of agony and anger at our current situation. I could see the conflict raging behind them.

"Please?" I begged. My raspy voice garbled and sold the urgency of my request.

He took in a deep, disapproving breath. A faint smile arched his lips upward as he reached into his pocket. He held in front of me the slender, white casing that I had worked for ten years to steer clear of. I reached out slowly with my undamaged left hand and brought it to my cracked lips. I squinted at the intense flame when he flicked the lighter and inhaled deeply. The old habit settled into my burning lungs with surprising ease.

He set the pack and lighter down in my lap and stood back up. I watched him lumber over to the quiet shovel as he began digging once again while I puffed away on the smoke. After so long being nicotine free, the sudden introduction into my already damaged system was having the affect I had hoped it would.

I was fully awake and pissed as hell. The old Tennessee country girl that was no stranger to a few bar fights after one too many beers was in full control. The smoke barreled through my fear and left only fury in its cloudy wake when I exhaled.

A plan was beginning to form as the fogginess of unconsciousness began clearing.

"Thank you, Sambo."

I saw him flinch, a shiver of hurt at my referring to him by the name I had called him ever since he was five. He didn't stop his work when he answered.

"For the smoke or for savin' you from being raped?" he replied. He tossed another shovelful of black dirt to the side.

"Both," I said while keeping my eyes locked on his. He broke the stare first and resumed his task.

"Number seventy-five, huh? What exactly does that mean, Sambo?"

"Well, we had this plan, you see. To make money off of desperate women who had more cash than brains. A cop's retirement pay ain't diddly-squat."

Oh, God. Steady. Show no fear.

"So, you and Jacob hunted women. He caught them, stole their cash and then killed them. That means your role is that of disposer, correct?" I said, flicking the spent butt across the expanse of the cave. I reached down and grabbed another.

"Yeah, that 'bout sums it up."

"How did you and Jacob hook up? He isn't from our neck of the woods," I said, my confidence rising with each answered question.

As long as I can engage him in conversation...I stand a chance.

"Oh, we know each other from way back. We went to the academy together down in Knoxville. He worked Internet crimes for Sutter County for a few years but then discovered he could make a better living on his own. He was one of those computer geeks who could do anythin' and everythin'.

"We ran into each other about three and a half years ago at Jimmy Joe's pub on Highway 75. He was sloshed and got a little too friendly with a waitress and my, um, dinner companion. Jimmy Joe had me show him the door. If he'da been anyone else, I'da arrested him that night but he was my friend. He asked for a smoke when we was outside, and I obliged. I can't really explain it, but I just felt like he needed an ear to jaw at, so I listened while he smoked. Turns out, he was out drownin' his pain and sufferin' that night. Same as me."

The shovel slammed into the ground; his anger overtook him. I swallowed the fear that was trying to creep up my throat.

Keep the veins full of ice, Mandy.

"What pain was that, Sambo?" I asked, already knowing the answer.

"Rejection from the woman I loved," he replied, his voice thick with emotion. He paused for a moment and turned his head away from me, low like he was praying. He wiped his eyes on the sleeve of his shirt before resuming his task. Realizing he was battling with his feelings, I tested the waters.

"Sambo, my ankle is numb. May I move it? And my knee, it's dislocated. Please, help me get it back in place. It's hard to talk with you when I'm in so much pain."

He stopped and looked at me, his eyes a mixture of compassion and irritation.

"Of course, Mandy. I don't want you to be uncomfortable before you go."

Gee, thanks you fucker. Your compassion is overwhelming. How about you just stop digging and let me go?

He put the tool of my destruction down and came over to me. His eyes were full of a variety of emotions as he knelt down and placed both of his filthy hands on each side of my knee.

"This is gonna hurt like hell. You ready?" he said, the compassion apparent in his quiet words. "Don't worry. I've done this a bunch of times. Take a deep breath and on the count of three..."

I gritted my teeth, nodded my head, and sucked in a lungful of air.

"Ready."

"One, two, *three!*"

With a quick jerk, he popped my kneecap back into place. I couldn't stop the scream of agony that erupted out of me. It took all of my strength to remain conscious as waves of searing pain barreled through me. I was thankful for the cold cave wall, which helped keep me awake and cool the red hot burn that rushed throughout my system.

"Sorry, I know that hurts like a sonofabitch. Popped mine out twice in high school during football games. Remember that, Mandy? You and Shawna had to help me walk home and you held my hand. What a sweet day that was. You were so caring. I believe that was the day you decided to become a nurse, when you saw how your compassion affected others. Ah, memories. Soon, they will be all I have left."

He patted my hand with a reassuring touch and I had to force myself not to jerk my hand away. He stood up and went back to the hole, his steps slower than before.

Over his shoulder he said, "You should be feeling the relief by now." A seemingly heartfelt smile appeared. I concentrated on my revulsion to his touch and his voice to keep from passing out.

Focus, Mandy. Keep him talking.

"Now, let's quit talkin' 'bout the past. You asked me a question about my role in this, so I'll answer. My job in this game is the last, but most important one. I make sure the bodies are never found." Samuel lowered his head and began ripping through the dirt at a swift pace.

I bent my left leg up which helped ease the tightness in my chest with each breath. He was right--the pain was but a fleeting memory now. I scrunched my back tighter against the smooth wall, which helped stabilize my position on the floor. Head cleared and fury back in control, I lit another smoke and continued my questions. I was unwilling to acknowledge his brief moment of humanity in fixing my knee, so I honed in on our location.

"Well, it seems you found the perfect hiding spot." I glanced around at the makeshift graves. "A cave for God's sake. It seems rather dramatic. It's cold in here. I'm guessin' we aren't in Tennessee anymore?"

"Good catch, Mandy. You'da made a great cop."

"Seventy-four women are buried under those mounds of dirt, huh? Guess that means you two have been at this game for quite some time."

Samuel's head never moved. His remorseful eyes seemed unwilling to meet my inquisitive ones.

"Comin' up on nearly three years. And I'm no dolt, Mandy. I may not be the shiniest apple in the cart, but I am a good cop. I know how to hide evidence, that's for sure. Dad and I stumbled upon this cave on a huntin' trip when I was about eight. The hills of Kentucky are full of them. No one knows it's here. Don't no one come back this deep, not even the moonshiners. We only dis-covered it when we was a runnin' from a pop-up thun-derstorm. Took us three days to find our way out and back to our truck."

Kentucky? Jesus, what day is it? How long have I been out?

"Three years? You two have been rather busy bad boys, haven't you?" He didn't respond to that ques-tion. I could see a faint glow of pink from his cheeks. I wasn't certain that was from the exertion of digging or embarrassment.

"So, how exactly did the game work?"

"It's rather complicated, so I will give you the short version since I'm almost done. You see, the guy you know as Jacob, well that ain't his real name, by the way. It's Russell Martin. It's just one of the hundreds of iden-tities he had. As I said earlier, his heart was broken by a spiteful ex-wife. She left him and his bank account, high and dry. She'd hired her some high falutin' lawyer from Knoxville that took him for all he was worth. He'd just written the final check to her the night we reconnected at Jimmy Joe's. We talked at the bar for hours. I convinced Jimmy Joe into letting him come back inside, and we had us a nice little chat. That's when he explained this plan he was workin' on."

Just listen. Nod your head and listen.

"You see, earlier that day, he had just found out that his ex had this online dating profile and was braggin' about how much money she had from her divorce. *His money.* He was furious and wanted revenge. He decided that he would put his hacker skills to good use and make him some money. He knew he couldn't go after his ex because he would be considered the prime suspect, so he decided to go after other women. Lonely women that had recently become rich off of the hard work of their ex-spouses, figuring he could search online for new cash cows to hook up with. I'll admit, at first I was shocked, but the more he explained how easy it would be and the drunker I got, well, guess I kinda got sucked in."

"Are you telling me that you just forgot all about the law you took an oath to uphold and just decided that stealin' and killin' sounded like a good idea?" I said, immediately wishing I could retract the words. The last thing I wanted to do was piss him off. To my surprise, he laughed.

"Hell no! Killin' was never part of the game plan. I mean, he was just supposed to grab some quick cash from each one and move on. At first, I helped him by wading through tons of dating sites, trollin' for freshly divorced fish, but I ain't all that computer savvy. He was smart. He insisted that we never look for women from our own backyard. We hunted all over the country."

And saved the hometown gal for the final one.

"But the first one, well, she looked just like his ol' lady, and I guess he lost control. He called me in a drunken panic one night, and when I arrived, he took me to her, um, remains in his barn. I knew there was no turnin' back then because I was in too deep. And Jacob, er, Russell, discovered he enjoyed killin'. Got a real taste for it. Sometimes, he would keep the women in his barn for days, doin' all sorts of unspeakable things. The more pain he caused, the more they offered for their life. So, that's when I just became the clean-up guy. When he was done with 'em, he called me and I came and picked up the…bodies. No one knows about this cave 'cept me."

The hole was getting bigger as Samuel's movements were spurred on by the memories. A wave of nausea swept over me as I glanced back over my shoulder to the silent victims.

"Jacob must have been quite the computer expert if he covered his tracks for so long. And picking your victims from all over, that was a smart move. No wonder their disappearances haven't all been linked together. And the two of you split the booty fifty-fifty from these women, and seventy-five victims was your limit. What, did Jacob get greedier and you decided to kill him?"

"I told you, that was *my* magic number. I got enough cash now to live high on the hog for the rest of my life. Besides, it had to end sometime, and someone had to take the fall. I didn't like all this death, but I sort of was stuck, ya know? But once we figured out how to pin it all on Jacob, err, Russell, we saw the light at the end of the tunnel. He had the looks and the charm to lure the ladies but not much going on in the brain department outside of being a hacker. Russell couldn't carry on a conversation worth a lick of salt, know what I mean?"

We?

"Yeah, he was charming online but sort of a dork in person, at least from my perspective on the other side of the dinner table," I said sarcastically. "There were no sparks, that's for sure. Guess I didn't fall prey to his deadly ways."

"No, but he got you anyhow. On the highway."

"Let me guess. He sabotaged my tire when he went to the bathroom?"

"Yeah, he did," Samuel replied as he slung more dirt.

"No wonder he was gone so long. Gee, and I just assumed he was calling a friend to tell them how great the date was going."

Samuel chuckled and his inappropriate laughter made me want to scream. "You always did have a bitter sense of humor, Mandy. I'm sure gonna miss it."

I smiled wickedly at him in response and lit another cigarette. At least our conversation was buying me time to consider all of my options. He wasn't looking in my direction any longer, so I stole a quick glimpse of the layout of the cave. It was difficult to make much out since the only light was coming from the lantern by his feet. I had no idea how far the entrance of the cave was from my position. The only thing I did know was which direction I would claw my way to once I figured out a way to escape.

Samuel stood six two and the ceiling was considerably higher, maybe twelve feet. The width was about twice that size and the depth unknown. Obviously, it was far enough to bury nearly a hundred women.

And that's when I caught a glint of something red and metallic. It rested near the spot I had been before Sam moved me. Christ, why didn't I think to search for it before?

It was my purse which held my gun.

Hallelujah!

"I doubt you will miss my sense of humor any more than I will miss dishing it out. So, tonight was the end. The last trinkets stolen and thrown into your coffers, all ready to pin it on Jacob, the unwilling patsy. Was he going to get his fifty percent of my money too, or were you going to keep all that yourself? You know, since we're practically like brother and sister, to keep the cash in family, so to speak?"

Sam kept shoveling as sadness and regret spread across his face.

"I told you, Mandy. Seventy-five was the perfect number. It was easier since we split the um, er, proceeds three ways. But tonight, Jacob wasn't gettin' a dime. The money was only going to be halved."

Three ways? We? Oh God, there was another…

I nodded in agreement and motioned for him to continue, my heart pounding at the discovery of another partner. I swallowed the bile that was making its way up my esophagus. What if the other partner showed up? And who the hell was it? If I survived, would I be forced to spend the rest of my life looking over my shoulder, worried about them finding me?

"We made sure that everything points back to him. All the money was funneled into his bank account. Then large sums of cash withdrawn and given to us. I never put mine in the bank. It's hidden inside my gun safe at home. No paper trail, no siree Bob. I told you, tonight was the last night. I'm just sorry that you're the last one."

"Yeah, but not as sorry I am." That reply brought a small grin to his sweaty face. "I assume, since I met Jacob on a dating site, that's the hunting ground you all used?" Since he was being so forthcoming with information, I hoped I could get him to tell me about the third partner.

He nodded silently, the intensity back with a vengeance. The hole was getting deeper.

My internal wheels were spinning. I had to figure out a way to get to my gun without him noticing.

"He picked out women who had money, right?" Again, he gave me a nod of agreement, his hair bouncing in harmony with the movement. "But I'm not rich. I'm a nurse for God's sake."

Samuel paused in mid-shovel and stared at me with a look of pity. The kind of look you would give a child while they tried to figure out a difficult homework problem. You know they know the answer, so you wait while their brain runs through the calculations and finally solves the puzzle.

Neurons fired on all cylinders and the answer slapped me in hard the face. My huge divorce settlement from Scott had netted me close to one point five million.

"I never told him about my divorce settlement, so why did he choose me?"

He stopped shoveling for the last time. The hole was dug. My grave prepared. He leaned against the shovel, his eyes full of sadness as he wiped his sweaty brow with a bandana he had pulled from his back pocket. Then, to my horror, he noticed my purse and stepped over to it. In one swift movement, he tossed it down into the hole.

My heart sank when I didn't hear a thud, which meant he already found my gun and disposed of it.

"Mandy, really, you don't wanna know. Please, drop it. Go to the next life without that answer. It will only hurt you more. And I don't want to be the one to tell you. It's hard enough on me, knowing I am the one killin' you." I heard the hitch in his voice. A small crack as the emotional weight of what he was about to do hit him. "I have loved you my whole life, and this is the hardest thing I've ever had to do. But, business is business, and I ain't got no choice. I don't plan on spendin' my remainin' years behind bars, not even for the woman I love. Cops behind bars don't last long."

My mind spun out of control--my hopes dashed. While I watched his face contort with emotion, I dug through my memories of the last three years. My divorce records with Scott were sealed. The last two hundred and fifty thousand had been deposited less than a week ago into my account. When Scott caught me in the break room at work and informed me he didn't owe me "a fucking dime" anymore, the conversation had not been a pleasant one. He had complained about his finances and the fact that he couldn't afford to get his newest squeeze anything nice or take her on vacation for her upcoming birthday. I remembered laughing at him, telling him that if he had kept his dick in his pants, we wouldn't be having this conversation. That, of course, pissed him off even more.

Not even my mother knew of the massive settlement I received since it was rolled directly into a trust. No one knew except my best friend. Sam's sister, Shawna.

My childhood comrade. Maid of honor at my wedding and the woman whose shoulder I cried on for weeks after my divorce. The girl that I held tight while she sobbed at the loss of both of her parents less than one year apart. My friend that I moved into my spare room for two months while I nursed her back to health after a horrible car accident because she didn't have insurance to cover home health care. A car accident that happened three years ago — the same time that Sam and Jacob began their game. The bouncy, effervescent creature who could make me laugh at life, no matter how grim the situation seemed.

Shawna was dating a man that she refused to tell me much about, preferring to keep things secret, which was completely out of character for her. A hush-hush sort of thing because she said he was a divorced man who insisted upon keeping his identity a secret while he dealt with an overbearing, money hungry ex-wife. She kept that promise to her new mate and only fed me scraps of information about him for the past two months.

Oh God, why did I not see it before? How did I miss that she was screwing Scott...

Which made her the third member of the deadly trio. Dear God...

My head spun as all the pieces finally came together. Betrayed by the person I was closest to in the entire world. Hot, fresh tears followed the dirtied tracks of the previous ones, and this time, I let them flow without restraint.

"Shawna?" I said, my voice choked with pain.

"Dammit Mandy, you never could accept no for an answer, could you? Yeah, Shawna set the whole thing up. I'm sorry I lied to you earlier. I *did* know before I got to the Chancery Court that you were Russell's date, but I swear I didn't find out until two hours before.

"You see, Shawna and Russell always orchestrated the game. She found them online, befriended them and learned their secrets. Social media — it's a place that people seem to think they make real friends, real bonds, real connections. And I guess sometimes that is the case, but for Shawna and Russell, it wasn't. She would laugh when she talked about how much information strangers were willing to give out online, especially from women who had money, but were lonely and searching for love. She picked 'em, contacted Russell, and we let him do his thing. Both of 'em know all 'bout that hacker stuff. They kept their trails wiped clean. I was just called in at the last minute to, well, clean up the mess."

I dropped the nearly spent smoke. The sobs of sorrow and physical pain overcame me. I doubled over and wept the tears of despair that only come from ultimate betrayal and impending death. My left hand fell down to my boot, hitting something hard as I tried to wrap my arm around my leg and pull myself into a tight ball. A last ditch effort to comfort my wounded soul.

"Shawna even told me about the gun in your purse, you know, to warn me so you wouldn't shoot me or somethin'. She said you were sneaky like that, but I told her you were just smart. At least you *tried* to be safe but guess you was so wrapped up in your date, you forgot to bring it. I'm sorry, Mandy. I really am, but time's up. It's almost daylight and I need to leave under the cover of darkness. Don't worry though. I'll make this quick and painless."

I heard the shovel clank when he released his grip and his footfalls drew closer. That sorry bitch may have warned him about the gun that *was* in my purse-- which was her fucking idea--but, I had completely forgotten that I moved it to my boot until I felt the bulge--and it wasn't there at her suggestion.

It had been *my* idea.

My momma didn't raise no fool. Damn straight.

While Samuel made his slow death march over to me, I eased my hand inside my boot and leaned to the left at the same time. My fake fainting spell worked and my fingers were firmly wrapped around the cold steel.

"That's a good girl, Mandy. Keep those beautiful eyes closed and rest now. I promise...I will drink a cold one for you later in your honor. Such a shame — I would have made a damn fine husband to you, too." He cooed the last words into the silent cave. I sensed his body was close enough.

Cold anger spread through me, freezing any hesitation. I was completely detached from any emotional connection to the situation. Fury rose with me as the will to live smothered everything else.

"Fuck you, Sambo," I said, and fired. Powdery white smoke plumed out of the hole in my boot. The red hot muzzle burned my skin as I pulled the revolver free. The sound reverberated throughout the cave and my ears rang from the concussion. Pain from my movements and the burn ripped through me, but my instincts pushed them to the side.

Surviving was front and center. Nothing more, nothing less.

The first bullet tore through his thigh, which caused him to spin just a fraction. He nearly lost his balance, his hands instinctively clasped around the wound, and his body bent over in shock and agony.

His body leaned closer. The face I had known since childhood clouded over in pain, eyes full of bewilderment and shock. I saw the look of dread in his face when he heard the hammer engage again.

The second bullet landed dead center, his heart shredded by the molten lava fragments that passed through him. The force knocked him back a few steps from me which gave me the time necessary to click the hammer back and take steady aim. The third one split the small space between his eyebrows, followed by a small trickle of red that dribbled down his nose. Terror, and a slight tremor of relief, crossed his face as he fell backward on top of the dirt he had excavated for my grave. His life was over before he hit the ground.

CHAPTER 2

"YOU'RE ONE LUCKY woman, Ms. Russell."

The young detective at the edge of my hospital bed closed his notepad and smiled at me. He was doing his best not to look like he just won the lottery at my expense. I wanted to be angry with him, but I couldn't. Hell, if I were in his shoes, I would be happy too. Even though there were seventy-four victims to be identified and families to be given a final answer as to the whereabouts of their missing loved ones, the reign of terror was over.

"Well, I'm not sure if lucky is the appropriate word for what I am feeling right now, but thank you anyway."

"Well, call it what you like, but in my book, you are. And a hero. Think of all the lives you saved from suffering the same fate that you almost did. You stopped the slaughter of more women from two heartless killers. Plus, once we have a chance to call in a forensic accountant to put together a complete financial workup on the finances of the perps, what funds are determined to belong to the victims will be sent back to the surviving family members. Not that they wouldn't trade the cash for their loved ones back, but at least it's something. Closure, if there is such a thing."

Closure. I suppressed a cynical laugh at that statement. There wasn't such a thing, not after the horrors inflicted by the deadly trio.

I stared down at my bandaged body, buried amidst the piles of blankets in the bed. It was my third day in the hospital in Crenton, Kentucky, which was over two hundred miles from Bainsville. The last seventy-two hours had been a blur of highs and lows.

I survived the painfully long journey out of the cave to Samuel's car outside that took me hours to accomplish in the shape I had been in. Like a zombie, I staggered through the twisting cave, eventually forced to crawl when the lantern burned out. Claustrophobia set in and a few times, I just stopped and waited for death, unable to overcome my sorrow and fear. Twice I curled into the fetal position and stared into the dark nothingness, waiting to be swallowed up by the black hole I seemed doomed to be trapped in.

But then, just as I began to succumb to the siren's whisper to close my eyes and drift away, the voices of the dead urged me on. I couldn't let those women be lost in the cave any longer, so I pushed on despite the odds that were stacked against me. When I caught the first glimpse of sunlight, I ignored my bloodied feet, hands, and knees and ran, almost as though the light infused me with healing strength.

The first full breath of fresh air I sucked in with fervor, ignoring the tremendous pain it caused my chest. I squinted under the intensity of the early afternoon sunbeams, desperate to find my car. Had I been able, I would have jumped for joy when I spotted it about fifty yards from me, hitched right behind Samuel's truck.

Relief washed over me when I found the door unlocked and my phone in the front seat, but that triumph had quickly sunk to dejection when I realized it was dead. Elation jolted me alive once more when I glanced through the window of Samuel's truck and noticed a CB radio under the dash. The tears that I held inside me broke free when I discovered it worked. My raspy voice screamed across the airwaves for help.

A flash of blue lights, the squall of sirens, a bumpy helicopter evacuation to the hospital, and countless hours of questions from law enforcement occupied two full days. The first day I experienced a gut wrenching phone call to my mother that damn near broke my heart. I had feared she would suffer another stroke, which had been at the forefront of my mind when I called. I made sure my words were chosen carefully as I downplayed my injuries.

I had to pull out every trick in the book I knew to keep her and Dad from coming up here. The last thing I wanted was for either of their weakened eyes to attempt to navigate the mountain roads or see their only child in such a condition. I told Dad to keep the television off and not answer any phone calls or visits from the press. I told him to have Mom occupy her time fixing me pre-pared meals that I could just heat up since cooking with broken fingers might prove difficult. Finally, I promised them that once I left the hospital, I would stay with them a few days while I recuperated. Parental worries placat-ed, they relented and stayed home.

I had told numerous law enforcement officials every sordid detail, from beginning to end, several times.

Well, *not everything.*

I omitted one large, particular detail.

A detail I would handle on my own once I returned home.

The wounds to my body would heal eventually. My knee was still tender, my fingers taped together, seven

stitches in my skull, and my ribs still sore with each res-
piration. The fluids delivered to me intravenously had
rehydrated my parched body, but the trauma embedded
inside my soul…that was another thing.

Another thing indeed.

"Ms. Russell, are you okay? Do I need to call the
nurse? You look like you are in pain."

I smiled up at the detective in response.

"I'm sorry. Guess I sort of zoned out for a moment. I
was just thinking about closure," I said. He nodded som-
berly, no more explanation needed.

"And no, thank you, calling the nurse is not necessary. I'm just ready to go home. I want to see my family.
And to forget about all this…this nightmare."

"Of course you are. Once you are released, I will
be driving you back to Bainsville. I'm sure your family
can't wait to see you. Let me go check on your release
papers, and then we will be on our way. Okay?"

I nodded in appreciation. It was against standard
hospital protocol for anyone other than a duly qualified
family member or an ambulance to transport a patient
home. Of course, Crenton was even smaller than Bainsville and rules were meant to be broken. If I had to guess,
I would say that Detective Milton wanted to pick my
brain on the drive back, maybe to see if I remembered
anything else that might be of use to them. Then again, it
could be that he just wanted my perception of cops to be
less tainted after almost being buried alive by one.

"Yes, and I can't wait to see them. And my best
friend. I can't imagine how upset Shawna is after not
only losing her brother but finding out he was a serial
killer, err, burier."

The detective's eyes clouded over, I'm sure from the disgust of knowing that a fellow officer was involved in such a despicable crime. The fraternal bonds of the blue were deep, and when one brother strayed from the fold, they all seemed to feel the pain and humiliation.

"Yes, as we all are. Hard to believe one of us could be such a monster. Tarnishes the badge for us all."

"One bad seed doesn't taint the entire apple, detective," I replied, his smile of gratitude real. "Did you happen to find out when the funeral is?"

"It is scheduled for tomorrow at two. Are you planning on attending?" he asked, his face devoid of emotions but his voice carrying a hint of incredulity.

I sighed heavily and looked out the window. A hot tear slid down my face and landed on my lap. "I don't know. I am very conflicted about that. I want to be there for Shawna. Samuel was all the family she had left. Now she will be rattling around that big ol' house they shared all alone. I can't fathom the mental anguish she must be experiencing. But, I'm really worried about how the fact that I shot him will affect our relationship and my presence at his funeral. The pain of losing a loved one doesn't lessen no matter what the circumstances of their departure were, and sitting next to her brother's executioner might be too much for her to handle."

"Well, I can't offer any sort of advice in that area, but I can tell you that she has called the nurses' station several times to check on you. I doubt that she would be interested in your welfare if she didn't still care about you, Ms. Russell."

Ha, if he only knew!

I let a feeble smile tug at the corner of my lips and focused my attention to his face. I reached out with my hand for his, which he eagerly clasped.

"Thank you for telling me that Detective Milton. Maybe there is hope our friendship can be salvaged after all."

His warm hand patted mine with one awkward touch. He quickly let go as a flush of embarrassment crept into his face.

"I hope my knee holds out for our, um, my trip. God, funny how life is all about timing—on the dot or way off the mark."

Detective Milton cocked his head slightly in curiosity.

"Oh, I booked us a tropical vacation getaway for her birthday. It was to be a surprise. Shawna always wanted to go to the Caribbean. She just never could afford it. Fortunately, I can. I was hoping the scenery would be a welcome salve to the atrocity of turning forty. You know, us gals have a thing about that number. Youth has officially passed and nothing left to look forward to except old age. Maybe, if she still wants to go, it will help her get over this. I know it will help me heal."

"I'm sure after the initial shock wears off, things will calm down. Now, let's get you home so you can rest," he said. He turned his back and disappeared, his feet carrying him at a brisk pace out to the nurses' station.

I shifted my weight on the hard mattress so I could look out the window. A vibrant blue sky dotted with fluffy white tufts of clouds sat in somber silence. The serene view did nothing to quench my smoldering anger as my thoughts of Shawna swirled around in my mind.

Yes, a vacation hiking on the jagged, remote cliffs on the islands with my *best friend* was definitely in order.

Jacob and Samuel may have been numbers seventy-five and seventy-six, but that didn't count. After all, it had been women that were the hunted game.

And I sure as hell knew which female was in my sights for number seventy-five.

I watched the clock tick precious seconds away. I had the perfect murder plotted and ready to execute. The ironic part was that I had already had the vacation to Dominica booked so there would be nothing suspicious about the trip. Two tickets--one for me and one for Shawna--and a weeklong stay at a bungalow right on the water. I had planned on telling her at dinner the night after my date with Jacob. The best part was that my mother was in on the secret and had actually gone with me the day I went into Knoxville to arrange everything.

And now, a cop knew.

I had the perfect alibis.

I didn't know much about police procedure and zip about accounting, but eventually, Shawna's role in the deadly game would be discovered. And that didn't need to happen until I had already killed her.

I could barely contain my eagerness from displaying across my face, and I had to force my fingers still. I was antsy, ready to get this show on the road and to show my friend a killer time in Dominica.

CHAPTER 3

THE AIRPLANE RIDE was long and uncomfortable, even in first class. In the three weeks since my attack, my knee was back to normal and my fingers were mending remarkably well. But my ribs still bothered me when confined to one position for too long. No wonder. Four of them were cracked, and although I wore a calm exterior, my insides were a knotted mass from stress. All that tension wasn't helping my muscles relax.

"I still can't believe we're here. My God, it's even more beautiful in person," Shawna gushed as we stepped out of the plane. The tropical air Dominica was known for greeted us with its heaviness, settling upon us like a hot, damp towel.

"Those glossy travel magazines just don't compare to the real thing, do they?" I said as we climbed down the stairs, inhaling the pungent air. "I can't wait to see the ocean."

"Oh, me either! I wonder if you can really see down hundreds of feet to the bottom like the travel brochure said. I mean, wow, that will be awesome! Nothing at all like the dirty lakes at home. Jesus, you can't see six inches below the surface. No telling what monsters are lurking about under your feet." Shawna laughed as we walked across the tarmac.

"Another reason I prefer crystal clear pools to swim in. Less worry about what lies beneath."

My fake laughter sounded so foreign to my ears because all I felt on the inside was dormant fury. Like the volcanoes that created Dominica eons ago, my hatred for my former best friend bubbled and churned, waiting impatiently to erupt. The façade of concerned friend, one who truly wished to mend the broken heart of her distraught best friend, was making me nauseous.

We hailed a cab and silence ensued between us as we each stared out the windows at the breathtaking scenery. I smiled and thought about paradise. Shawna certainly wasn't headed there when she departed this world, so I guess she would have to settle for dying in it. At least her final resting place wouldn't be in some dank cave. She was lucky.

I felt the apprehension seeping from her. I knew her mind was plotting my death just as mine was hers. Our minds both burned into overdrive as we each neared the end of our races. Simpatico sisters we were, but only one of us knew that.

I had been on guard ever since Detective Milton had driven me home to Bainsville. The ride home had been quiet, and my previous assumption that he had offered me a lift stemmed from his eagerness to continue questioning me had been way off base. He had been quiet and just let me think, only talking if I spoke first. I had pretended to doze off a few times and just let my brain wander, the inner beast called revenge had fully taken control. But that monster also was keenly aware that another predator was in its territory. A stealthy slayer that wanted revenge for her brother's death and my money.

Too bad she would not experience either.

Shawna had circled me like dinner when I arrived back home and turned her predatory growls into loving coos. She gushed. She cried. She apologized for what her brother had done to me. She thanked me for being strong enough to stand by her side while she said her final goodbyes to him. She even publically announced that I was all the family she had left, and we would lean on each other for emotional support during this sorrowful time. Heartfelt words were choked out from the pulpit at her brother's funeral so *everyone* would hear her speak of her love and devotion to me.

She marveled at my strength and will to live and to have escaped the clutches of death. She swooned with mock horror every time the news reported on the case and managed to shed a few real tears when her brother's face appeared on the screen. We talked on the phone and the night I told her about her surprise birthday trip to Dominica, she howled with delight. And why shouldn't she have? I had just handed her the opportunity to plan a tragic accident during our vacation.

It was obvious to me that she was trying to figure out exactly what I knew, what I didn't know, and what my weaknesses were so she could plan accordingly.

Both of us were living the old adage about keeping your friends close but your enemies closer. Hell, we were so close we could have shared the same skin. She did her best to hide her anger, careful to control her voice, her facial muscles, and her words when around me. But the eyes aren't so easy to control. Her performance was impeccable to others around her.

But I saw right through it, perhaps because I was playing the same role on the other side of the theater.

The press hounded us both for blood like a hungry tick does when looking to hitch a ride on the ol' huntin' dog. When they discovered the strange twist that involved our friendship, they were relentless. My father made national news when he was caught on film standing on his front porch early one foggy morning a few days after I arrived back. His hair had been mussed and his eyes full of anger as he clutched his shotgun in his hand and told the brazen young reporter from New York to get the hell off of his land.

There was nowhere to hide from their pesky intrusion, so all of us, including most of the population of Bainsville, just hunkered down in our homes and waited for the skirmish to end. The local restaurants mysteriously ran out of food when reporters walked in. The two motels were suddenly full. Doors remained closed and mouths shut.

I would lie awake at night locked like a prisoner in my house and peek through the blinds, waiting for the moment they packed up their shit and left after hitting the "small town" wall that had been erected. That didn't happen quickly enough for me--or the entire town--so I took a proactive stance and let the bloodsuckers feast for a few minutes. I held an impromptu press conference on my front porch and gave them what they wanted — the gory details.

Soon after, the annoying trucks lumbered out of town, off to intrude and invade on the lives of the next poor "headline" newsmaker. A collective sigh of relief swept through the town when the last van disappeared out of sight.

But not through me.

I had taken a leave of absence from my job at Mercy General, unsure when, if ever, I would return. Sleep evaded me. It had been replaced by continuous pacing inside the walls of my home. My emotions ran the gamut, flipping violently from one end of the spectrum to the next. When the betrayal took center stage, I felt the urge to grab my parents and simply move to another town; away from the agony and memories of what happened. Away from the torture that continuously ripped at my heart, knowing my near death was orchestrated by my closest friend. Add on top of that, the shame I felt from not only joining a dating site, but then the stupidity of meeting a stranger face to face. I struggled with not only the betrayal, but my feelings of humiliation.

Another fun emotion that visited often was guilt. I had been a caregiver my entire career. I had devoted my being to saving lives, not taking them. I didn't know how to live with the fact that I killed Samuel, even if it was thrust upon me in a split second, life-or-death situation. Kill or be killed didn't ease the heavy sense of remorse for his death. The Bible didn't leave an exclusionary clause under the commandment "Thou Shalt Not Kill." I had been grappling with that baggage, so how would I handle actually plotting out and committing cold-blooded murder? Would my psyche survive? Would my soul be forever damned?

Then the rage would take over. As the red-hot fury burned through my thoughts, it wiped out everything in its path. This wasn't just about me or my pain. There were seventy-four women who silently screamed for vengeance from their graves. Seventy-four women murdered and whose families now wore the permanent scar of their untimely and violent death. Seventy-four mounds of black dirt that haunted my dreams. These women deserved for me to be their voice of justice, so my rage won out and smothered all the other emotions in one giant gulp.

The cab pulled into the entrance of our bungalow, the jarring stop shaking me back to reality. My decision had been made, and the time had come to execute it.

"My God, Mandy. This place is amazing! You spared no expense, did you?"

I smiled as we exited the car.

"Nope. I wanted this to be the vacation of a lifetime!"

:●●

THE FIRST TWO days were spent frolicking on the beach, drinks in hand and backs slathered with oil. While our skin cooked to a deep copper brown, our conversations were minimal and topics lighthearted. The deeper conversation that both of us secretly pined for would happen on our upcoming hike.

The hotel had put us in touch with a mountain guide who spent two hours telling us about our options. Which trail we should take. What we should expect to see on each one. He warned us of what dangers lurked on the steep climb, vehement that we not veer from the clearly marked path. We filled out the registration papers and each nodded and smiled, thanking him for the maps and headed back to our bungalow.

"I believe he thinks we are nuts for hitting the trail alone, but the last thing I want to hear is a chatty guide. I want to explore this place alone. With my best friend, of course."

"Oh, you bet. We're big girls and we can take care of ourselves. Besides," I said, grabbing my backpack off the couch and handing Shawna hers, "he gave me the creeps. Guess I'm still a bit wary."

A shadow of anger danced behind her blue eyes but quickly retreated. She slung her pack over her shoulders and then gave me a hug.

"Of course you are, hon. Who wouldn't be? Even I am, after all that has happened. But let's not talk about that now. Come on," she said, tugging me out the door, "Let's go explore! Wide open spaces baby!"

Ten minutes later, we were about to embark on our journey. We stood in front of the Waitukubuli Trail that would take us through the Morne Trois Pitons National Forest at the entrance of one of the most difficult climbs — Boiling Lake and Roseau Valley. It was early in the morning and the steam from the rainforest hung heavy around our feet. We each took turns hamming it up by the sign and snapped a picture of each other. We giggled at our luck since we were the only ones embarking on the rugged walk. We were just two happy tourists ready to explore the mountains filled with excitement around every bend.

The map said the hike generally took about six hours in total and the first stop was about an hour in and would have us standing at about 2,950 feet above sea level. The greatest perk was that it had a rocky outcrop that offered stunning views of the ocean and island. The small picture on the map was the perfect place to have our showdown. We both agreed that should be where we stopped and had something to eat.

I convinced Shawna to lead the way, acquiescing to her stronger sense of adventure than what I possessed. She agreed with a vibrant smile and led the charge to the peak. Sure enough, almost an hour later on the nose, we exited the deep canopy of the rainforest and found ourselves in the brilliant sun, the view of the island and shimmering waters panoramic.

"My God, ain't this just the shit! Look Mandy, you can see the other side of the island from here!" Shawna gushed.

I glanced up at my childhood friend, her giddiness real, not faked. A few strands of her thick, honey-colored hair escaped the messy bun on her head, the tendrils swaying in the breeze. Her lanky, five-foot-ten frame jumped up and down like a small child as she took in the surroundings. The smile on her face threw memories of our past in front of me, showering me with visions of our thirty-plus-year friendship. Weddings, funerals, birthdays, the prom, learning to drive, our first double date, our first rip-roaring drunk and hangover flashed by. The hours spent gabbing on the phone to each other. Our marathon conversations started out in our youth about dolls and clothes, finally graduating to guys, sex, college and children.

Oh Jesus, I can't do this.

The images of the woman I practically considered my sister disappeared, replaced by the graves and Samuel standing over the freshly dug one, ready to dispose of me like yesterday's trash--on the orders of his big sister.

My lump subsided, and my resolve roared back. The stifling tropical air that permeated our earlier climb and weighed down my shields was blown away by the brisk trade winds.

Yes, yes I can. And I will.

My chest throbbed and I tried to mask the pain from my heaving ribs with a sweaty smile. I moved over toward the outcropping of giant boulders and set down my backpack.

"This is simply Heaven. The air is the most intoxicating mix of scents that I have ever smelled. I wish I could bottle it. I'd make millions."

"Girl, you ain't kidding! It sure is nice to be out of that creepy forest. I knew at any minute a jaguar was going pounce on us. I really didn't like the idea of being a snack."

Shawna plopped her pack next to mine and started digging through it, letting out a small squeal when she found her water bottle.

"There are no big predators on this island, silly."

Well, except for the two of us.

"Well, I'm just glad to be out of there. It felt like a ton of bugs were crawling all over me."

"That's just sweat. You're positively soaked," I said, throwing her a towel from my bag. I began unloading the small blanket and sandwiches for our picnic, watching every move she made out of my peripheral vision. She was busy setting up her portable tripod for her camera at the edge of the rocks, finding it difficult to steady in the uneven terrain.

"Those are going to be great shots. Guaranteed postcard quality for sure. Images are always worth a thousand words, right?"

Tripod in place and steady, Shawna stood back and surveyed the visual. Satisfied she had the camera pointing in the perfect direction, she came over and sat down on the blanket and snatched a sandwich.

"Yep, they sure are. Just wait until I upload them on my blog. People will go crazy with jealousy."

"You and that computer—it's an addiction, isn't it? You spend more time online than a gamer."

"Um, you forget that I work from home. Of course I'm on the computer all the time. It's how I make my living."

I smiled at her while I took a bite from my apple and watched the puffy clouds in the distance merge together. They had turned from cotton ball white to dingy gray and the low rumbling of thunder was a warning that a storm was brewing.

I turned my attention back to Shawna. She wasn't doing a very good job of hiding her irritation. Her throat muscles tensed and her pulse throbbed in her temple. I knew it wasn't from our hike. She was ready to strike, but I was going to beat her to it.

"What exactly is it that you do online Shawna? I don't believe you've really shared that with me other than you design websites, which you started doing while you recuperated from your accident. You aren't hooking on the side for extra money, are you?" I laughed, knowing those words would strike an angry chord. The looks of shock followed by anger were shining like a beacon on her damp skin. She paused in mid-chew and just stared at me, her eyes searching my own to see what I was getting at.

"You're such a bitch, you know that, right?"

I threw my head back and laughed. "Takes one to know one. Isn't that what they say?"

"Hey, I never claimed to be anything but. So," she replied easing herself up off the blanket, "what about you? After your, um, *ordeal*, are you going to take any of those offers to hit the talk show circuit?"

I faked a stretch and stood up as well and chunked my apple core over the cliff to the waters below. "You know how much I hate those kinds of shows. No way. I have, however, been giving serious consideration to taking up the offer to write a book about it. Three publishers have contacted me already."

Shawna's eyes widened with shock, the black storm clouds that were moving in paled in comparison to the anger swirling behind her eyes.

"Are you serious? A book?"

"Yeah. The only problem with that option is writing that last chapter," I said, casually walking over to my backpack.

"Why is that?" Shawna replied, her voice shaky.

I reached inside my bag and pulled out the knife I bought at the gift shop the day before and turned and faced my former best friend.

"Because it hasn't happened yet."

Shawna's reaction was immediate. She took three halting steps back from me, her eyes wide with fear. It was the first time in my life that someone had actually cringed with fear at my presence, and it was rather intoxicating. She was only inches away from the huge rock that jutted out over the cliff.

"What…what are you talking about, Mandy?"

I gripped the bone handle tight in my left hand and squared my shoulders, my steps small as I made my way toward her.

"You know, Samuel was very talkative while he was digging my grave. Guess he felt the need to unburden his soul before he buried me. I learned some *very* interesting tidbits of information about you and your online activities, Shawna. Oh, and the fact that you've been fucking my ex-husband and decided that offing me was a better option than just telling me. Typical Shawna—always taking the easy way out."

"How…how did you…?" Shawna stuttered.

"I put the puzzle pieces together when you brother was digging my grave, you sorry bitch."

A large clap of thunder rolled around us as cooling drops of rain began to fall. Shawna was up against the rock now with nowhere to go except to climb up it or come through me. Every muscle in my body was ready, awaiting the fight. Shawna had always been a scrapper and she towered over me. But there was no fear on my end, only rage, so I was prepared to lunge. I had played the scenario out numerous times, trying to anticipate the responses from her. But the one that I hadn't considered is what she gave me.

Tears.

"Please Mandy, don't. You don't understand. Oh God, I'm so sorry."

"Sorry? For what? Stabbing me in the back by hooking up with Scott, luring seventy-four innocent women to their deaths, or for making me the seventy-fifth?" I growled, moving closer.

"Mandy, please, let me explain." She held up her hands in desperation, her feet quickly scaling up the rock, putting space between us.

"There is no explanation for pure evil, Shawna."

Thunder clapped again and the sprinkles turned to a downpour. I raised my voice over the ferocious storm.

"How did it feel, knowing the unbelievable amount of suffering those poor women went through because *you* put them on their path of doom? How in the hell did you sleep at night? Did it just become easier after each one? I guess since they were strangers you felt no remorse, huh? But I'm not a stranger, Shawna. I *was* your best friend. And you betrayed me in the most unspeakable of ways. Now, it's time to pay for that."

Openly sobbing now, Shawna reached the peak of the rock. I followed her footsteps and blocked her escape route.

"I never expected death to be the ultimate result. I just thought Russell would swindle them out of their money. When he killed the first one, Samuel and I were stuck. I had already given hundreds of names to Russell, so he just kept on killing. What were we supposed to do, Mandy? Go to the police?"

"You never should have started in the first place, Shawna. And yes, once the first life was taken, you should have done the right thing. But you didn't. You just kept on. What I want to know before I kill you is why me? Why did you decide I was to be the last one? Because of some average- sized dick that functions about half of the time? Were you that hard up for a lump to keep you warm at night? Seriously, you would have done better with a dog—they are much more loyal. But the part that hurts the most is that you should've told me you were in love with Scott. It probably would have ended our friendship, but isn't that better than killing me and stealing my money? *You were my friend!*"

Shawna was teetering at the edge, her body shaking uncontrollably.

"Mandy, I love you! You have no idea how hard I fought to change his mind! I didn't pick you, I swear. Scott did."

Her words ripped out what humanity was left inside me. Shredded to the very core, wrath became my guiding force. The storm that raged around us was nothing in comparison to the one that churned inside my soul.

"*What?*"

"He…he caught me one night on the computer. It was late. I thought he was sleeping. When he figured out what we were doing, he threatened to go to the authorities. I begged him not to. He agreed to keep quiet…as long as you were the next victim. He wanted it done before he made his last payment to you. I…I had no choice, Mandy. When Jacob couldn't convince you fast enough to meet him, Scott just went ahead and paid you, then backed me into a corner. He warned me that if we didn't get all the money in your account, he would blow the lid off of our scheme. I was trapped."

Fury burned through me. The fires of betrayal charred all reasoning.

"Trapped? *Trapped?* Don't talk to me about being trapped. Try waking up in a dark cave while you watch your grave being dug by your childhood friend. Then we can discuss the sensation of feeling trapped. You put me through hell on earth—for money. And Scott? Can't say that I am surprised he's involved in plotting my death. Of course, if you'd actually been *my friend* and not out scurrying around behind my back like some horny alley cat, Scott would never have had the opportunity to put you in that position. Guess I will just have to deal with him later, after I'm done with you. Now, you have two choices, Shawna. Jump, or face me. Either way, you're dead."

Her face contorted in anguish, her limbs frozen in place. Great sobs of agony spewed out of her as resignation to her dire situation hit home. She turned and glanced behind her at the steep drop to the craggy rocks and frothy water below. For a minute, I thought she was going to take the coward's way out.

The sobs suddenly dried up and her back straightened. A chill passed through me when I realized she chose to fight. The same determination to live that I had experienced in the cave exuded out of her like a palpable entity. I understood her gut instinct to survive, but it would be trumped by my animal instinct to kill.

I clung onto the soaking wet knife for dear life and crouched, ready for her assault. She spun around at the same time as a bolt of lightning slammed into the mountainside less than a hundred yards away. The concussion from the thunderclap that followed it shook the rock we stood upon and caused her to lose her balance on the slippery surface. Her arms spun in wild circles as she tried to maintain her footing, but it was no use. Her feet went out from under her, and she toppled over backward.

Her screams were drowned out as the storm barreled down around me. I dropped to my belly and crawled to the edge and watched her flailing body bounce like a ragdoll against the sharp rocks. In seconds, her mangled body came to a rest on the beach below, face down in the wet sand.

My anguished screams, borne from betrayal, loss and pain, were muffled by the swirling storm. The hot tears were indecipherable from the salty rain as I wept for the loss of the person I once was and the one I had become. They also were a cleansing release that Shawna's end was meted out by divine intervention and not from my own hands.

CHAPTER 4

"GOOD MORNING, MS. Russell. I have some news for you if you have a moment."

I was sitting in my kitchen, enjoying a cup of stout espresso after a long night of writing in my journal. Less than fifteen minutes before the phone rang, I had just finished the final scene from Shawna's demise in Dominica. The memories were still fresh and easily recalled since it had only been a month since that day on the rocks.

"Good morning, Detective Milton. I am already sitting down, so go ahead."

"Oh, I'm sorry. I should have prefaced that with I have some *good* news," he responded. His embarrassment seeped across the phone lines from Kentucky to Tennessee.

"Don't apologize. After everything that has happened, I just assumed it was bad. Guess I am a tad jaded."

"You sure have weathered some terrible storms, Ms. Russell. But I hope that my news will help bring some blue sky your way."

"Well, now that would be a welcomed change. I'm all ears."

"Number one is your gun has been officially released now that the case is closed. You are welcome at any time to come pick it up. Number two is that the forensic accountant finished the examination of the bank records. All the funds have been distributed evenly back to the families. They all asked me to express their heart-felt thanks for everything, and some requested that I pass along their prayers."

"I appreciate you letting me know, Detective. If you have a chance to speak to any of them again, please tell them thank you for me."

There was a moment of brief silence and I sensed he wasn't quite finished yet. I knew what subject he was trying to broach, so I beat him to it.

"I assume you heard that Scott entered a guilty plea yesterday and was sentenced to twenty years."

He tried to let his sigh of relief out quietly, but it didn't work.

"Yes, I heard. Guess he didn't want to risk a jury of his peers sending him away for life."

"Yeah, he always was a chicken shit," I said, laughing as I thought how his blonde hair and lithe frame would look like dessert to his new cell mates.

"I heard on the news the other day that you were writing a book about your experiences called *Number 75*. Is that true?"

"Sort of. I am putting all my thoughts down in a journal and then I am to deliver them to the publisher. They will have someone ghostwrite it—I believe that's what they called it. I just finished the last volume right before you called. Good thing too because I couldn't hold the pen any longer. My fingers are dead tired."

"You're writing out the story by hand? Wow, old school."

"I no longer own a computer, Detective. They are too dangerous."

"I can see why you would feel that way, Ms. Russell. So, would you like to schedule a time to come pick up your weapon?"

"To be honest Detective, I don't plan on setting foot inside the state of Kentucky ever again. Do what you wish with it. I have plenty here to keep me safe."

My momma didn't raise no fool.

Damn straight.

About the Author

INTERNATIONAL BESTSELLING AUTHOR, Ashley Fontainne, is an avid reader of mostly the classics. Ashley became a fan of the written word in her youth, starting with the Nancy Drew mystery series. Stories that immerse the reader deep into the human psyche and the monsters that lurk within us are her favorite reads.

Born and raised in California, Ashley now calls Arkansas home with her husband and four children. Her suspense series, Eviscerating the Snake, has received rave reviews for all three titles, *Accountable to None, Zero Balance* and *Adjusting Journal Entries.* She also enjoys writing poetry and short stories and recently published *Ramblings of a Mad Southern Woman: A Collection of Short Stories and Poetry on Life, Love, Loss and Longing,* which is available on Amazon. Ashley is also a supporter of the Joyful Heart Foundation that assists victims of violent crime seek help and find healing, and donates 10% of all book sales yearly to the cause.

Ashley invites you to visit her:

Website

www.ashleyfontainne.com

Blog:

ramblingsofamadsouthernwoman.blogspot.com

Twitter:

@AshleyFontainne